Recording produced and arranged by Janis Ian & Randy Leago
Engineered by Randy Leago; solo guitar/vocal version engineered by Gordon Hammond
Mastered by Independent Mastering, Nashville
Transcription by Luke Woodard

Cataloging-in-publication data is available.

ISBN 978-1-935954-30-9 (Hardcover)

Printed in the United States by Worzalla, Stevens Point, Wisconsin

First U.S. Edition

www.lemniscaatusa.com

www.thetinymouse.com

www.janisian.com

janis ian / rude girl pub.

Janis Ian

The Tiny Mouse

Illustrated by Ingrid & Dieter Schubert

LEMNISCAAT

There was a tiny mouse
who lived in a tiny house
full of drafts and doubts, and incredible things,

like a jack-in-the-box who popped
every Sunday at five o'clock
and a clown who wore a frown that was deafening.
He ate off a silver spoon
in a golden room
but platinum plates and diamond goblets weren't enough.

"I am bored," said he.
"I think I will go to sea
where I'll be drinking grog and sniffing occasional snuff."

So he stowed away that very day,

but the motion of the ocean made him sick.

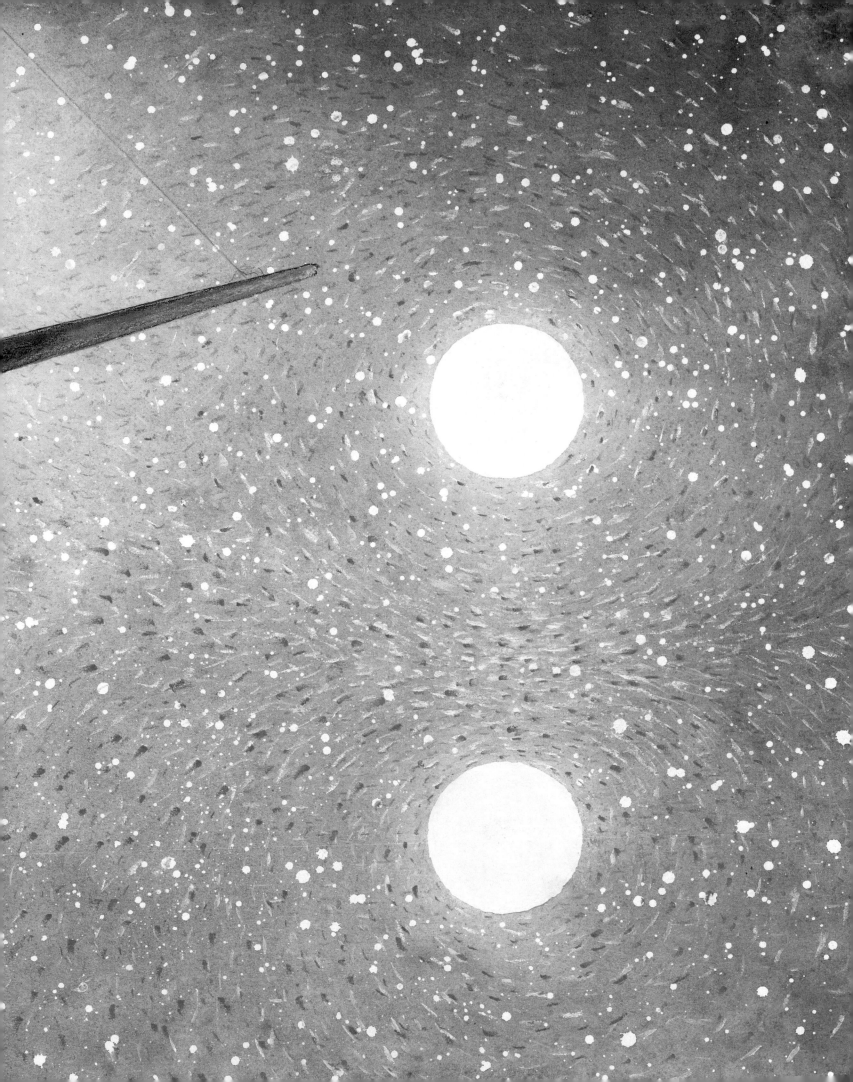

He went looking for a loo,
but the best that he could do
was the bathroom of the captain of the ship.

Oh, the bathroom of the captain of the ship!

There was a small still life
of the captain's wife
and what he saw there nearly brought the mouse to tears.
A calico coat and head
and the inscription read
"To the captain of my heart, from Kitty Dear."

The mouse began to cry
"Oh what a fool am I
to come so far and then be served up on a plate.
What an awful meal I'll be!
Most of all, to me!!
So it's overboard I'll go and make my escape."

He caught a flounder for a sail,
made rudder of his tail
and swam as hard as he could swim for land,

where he dried his whiskers off
and coughed and coughed and coughed
and spat out seven oysters and a clam.
Oh, he spat out seven oysters and a clam!

He married a mouseketeer,
had children who loved to hear
about the adventures of the tiny stowaway,
but it made their noses itch
and their whiskers twitch
to think how close he'd come to being the soup of the day.

The moral of the tale
is *think before you sail*
and always keep your paws and whiskers neat.
If you're dining on a ship
just be sure the room's well lit.
Always know what's in the bowl before you eat.
Always know what's in the bowl before you eat!!

The Tiny Mouse

Words and Music by
JANIS IAN

Steady (♩. = 108) **VERSE 1**

There was a tin-y mouse who lived in a tin-y house full of drafts and doubts and in-cred-i-ble

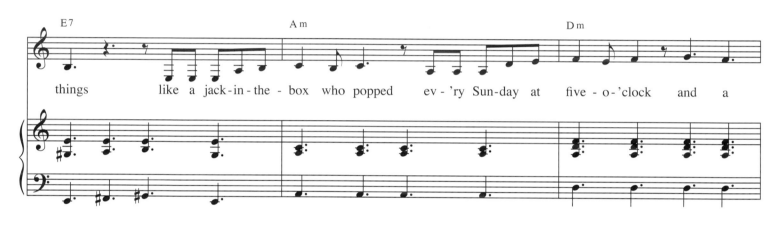

things like a jack-in-the-box who popped ev-'ry Sun-day at five-o-'clock and a

clown who wore a frown that was deaf-en-ing._____

VERSE 2

He ate off a sil-ver spoon in a gold-en room but plat-i-num

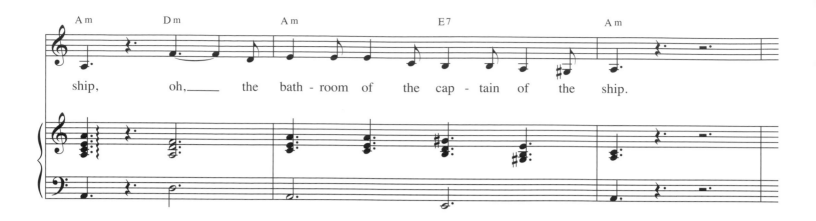

ship,   oh,____ the bath - room of   the cap - tain of   the   ship.

VERSE 3

There was a small still life of the captain's wife
And what he saw there nearly brought the mouse to tears.
A calico coat and head and the inscription read,
"To the captain of my heart, from Kitty Dear."

VERSE 4

The mouse began to cry, "Oh, what a fool am I
To come so far and then be served up on a plate!
What an awful meal I'll be – most of all to me!
So it's overboard I'll go and make my escape!"

CHORUS 2

He grabbed a flounder for a sail, made a rudder of his tail
And swam as hard as he could swim for land
Where he dried his whiskers off and coughed and coughed and coughed
And spat up seven oysters and a clam.
Oh, he spat up seven oysters and a clam.

VERSE 5

He married a mouseketeer, had children who loved to hear
About the adventures of the tiny stowaway.
But it made their noses itch and their whiskers twitch
To think how close he'd come to being the soup of the day.

CHORUS 3

The moral of the tale is think before you sail
And always keep your paws and whiskers neat.
And if you're dining on a ship, just be sure the room's well lit.
Always know what's in the bowl before you eat.
Always know what's in the bowl before you eat!